THEY'RE FAMOUSE . . .
THEY'RE FABUMOUSE . . .
AND THEY'RE HERE
TO SAVE THE DAY!
THEY'RE THE

HEROMICE

AND THESE ARE THEIR
ADVENTURES!

Geronimo Stilton

THE PERILOUS PLANTS

Scholastic Inc.

Published by Scholastic Inc., 557 Broadway, New York, NY 10012. SCHOLASTIC and associated logos are trademarks and/or registered trademarks of Scholastic Inc.

Stilton is the name of a famous English cheese. It is a registered trademark of the Stilton Cheese Makers' Association. For more information, go to www.stiltoncheese.com.

ISBN 978-0-545-93092-5

Text by Geronimo Stilton
Original title *Il superattacco delle margherite zannute*
Original design of the Heromice world by Giuseppe Facciotto and Flavio Ferron
Cover by Giuseppe Facciotto (design) and Daniele Verzini (color)
Illustrations by Luca Usai (pencils), Valeria Cairoli (inks), and Daniele Verzini (color)
Graphics by Chiara Cebraro

Special thanks to Shannon Penney
Translated by Julia Heim
Interior design by Kevin Callahan / BNGO Books

10 9 8 7 6 5 4 3   16 17 18 19 20

Printed in the U.S.A.   40

First printing 2016

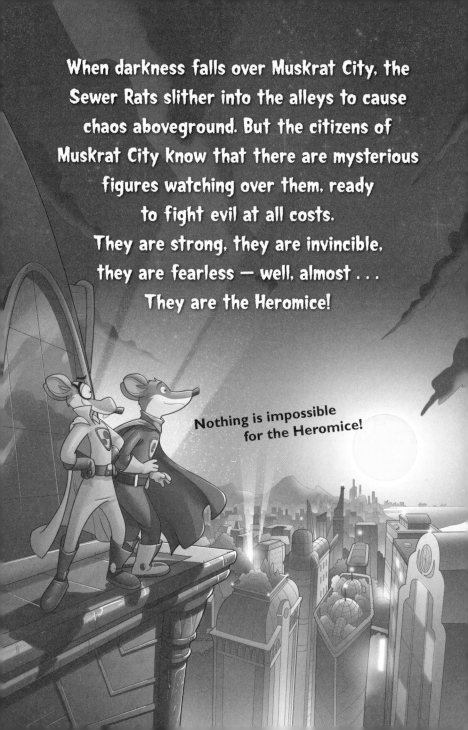

When darkness falls over Muskrat City, the Sewer Rats slither into the alleys to cause chaos aboveground. But the citizens of Muskrat City know that there are mysterious figures watching over them, ready to fight evil at all costs.
They are strong, they are invincible, they are fearless — well, almost . . .
They are the Heromice!

Nothing is impossible for the Heromice!

MEET THE HEROMICE!

GERONIMO SUPERSTILTON

The strongest hero in Muskrat City . . . but he still must learn how to control his powers!

SWIFTPAWS

Geronimo Superstilton's partner in crimefighting; he can transform his supersuit into anything.

LADY WONDERWHISKERS

A mysterious mouse with special powers; she always seems to be in the right place at the right time.

TESS TECHNOPAWS

A cook and scientist who assists the Heromice with every mission.

ELECTRON AND PROTON

Supersmart mouselets who help the Heromice; they create and operate sophisticated technological gadgets.

TONY SLUDGE

The undisputed leader of the Sewer Rats; known for being tough and mean.

AND THE SEWER RATS!

SLICKFUR

Sludge's right-hand mouse; the true (and only) brains behind the Sewer Rats.

TERESA SLUDGE

Tony's wife; makes the important decisions for their family.

ELENA SLUDGE

Tony and Teresa's teenage daughter; has a real weakness for rat metal music.

ONE, TWO, AND THREE

Bodyguards who act as Sludge's henchmice; they are big, buff, and brainless.

A GREEN-PAWED MOUSE

It was a **warm** spring day, and I was relaxing on the balcony of my home in New Mouse City. Ahhh, what a mouserific afternoon! The sun was shining, and a refreshing *breeze* blew through the city . . .

Oops, I'm sorry—I haven't introduced myself! My name is Stilton, *Geronimo Stilton*, and I'm the editor in chief of *The Rodent's Gazette*, the most **famouse** newspaper on Mouse Island.

It's an important job, and I usually have a CHEESELOAD of work to do, but that day I had finished early and was busy gardening.

I needed to pot, fertilize, and water my new plants, but first and foremouse, I had to talk to them!

No, I'm not out of my fur!

My Aunt Sweetfur is the best gardener in New Mouse City. She always says that talking to plants keeps them **happy**. And happy plants are healthy plants—rodent's honor!

With that in mind, I began whispering to the **roses**. "Little roses, you're already looking fabumouse! This sun will be good for you. It will help you grow *bigger* and **stronger**!"

"Hey there, Cuz!" someone hollered from the street. "Is everything all right? Are you talking to yourself?"

Oh, poor Gerrykins!

I looked down and . . . **hmph!**

I should have known. It was my cousin Trap!

"I'm fine, Trap. If you must know, I'm not talking to myself—I'm talking to my **PLANTS**!"

Trap gave me a confused look. "Oh, poor Gerrykins . . . all this sun on your fur must have hurt your brain!"

I watched my cousin as he walked off, **whistling**. Sigh! When he acts like this, Trap really **drives me cheesy**!

But this wasn't the time to let things get under my fur. After all, it was a beautiful spring afternoon! After I finished **gardening**, I had some delicious plans. I was going to munch on:

1) a yummy supersnack of **Parmesan** cheese chips;

2) a morsel of *Muenster* mousse;

3) a big bellyful of aged cheddar, plus a slice of lasagna with **MELTED MOZZARELLA**!

Holey cheese—just the thought of all that food made my mouth water!

As I was daydreaming about those delicious cheeses, the telephone rang.

RPPPING! RPPPPING!! RPPPPPING!!!

I jumped, and the watering can accidentally slipped from my paws. It flew through the air and landed right on my snout, wetting me from the ends of my whiskers to the tip of my tail!

SPLASH!

I shook off my soggy fur and answered the phone with a sigh.

There was a familiar voice on the other end of the line. It was my good friend Hercule Poirat!

Hmph!

"Hercule," I said. "How *nice* to hear from you! Are you all right?"

"**Super Swiss slices**, there's no time to waste, hero partner!" he cried urgently. "Get your tail to Muskrat City right away! We need you here—or rather, we need **Superstilton**!"

My throat got dry. "Y-yes, I mean . . . n-no, I mean . . . I'm not your **HERO PARTNER**, I'm Geronimo Stilton, and right now I'm busy watering my plants—"

"**WHat?**" Hercule squeaked. "Are you saying that you can't join a special Heromouse mission because you need to do your gardening?"

"Well, no . . . I mean, yes, basically, I . . ." I wasn't sure what to say.

"Enough chattering, Geronimo! You're needed here—**no excuses**!"

He hung up.

I sighed. **Holey cheese!**

Maybe I could have come up with another *excuse*, but nothing came to mind. Besides, if Muskrat City really needed Superstilton, how could I **refuse**?

Resigned, I pulled my **Superpen** out of my pocket and pressed the secret button under the clip. A second later, a green ray **surrounded me**, transforming me into Superstilton!

ZAP!

Mighty mozzarella, I'd never get used to that!

Before I could even **squeak**, my Heromouse costume carried me up into the sky at superspeed. Destination: Muskrat City!

"*Great gobs of Gouda!*" I squealed. "Heeeeeelppppp!"

AN UNEXPECTED GUEST

I arrived in Muskrat City in no time, darting between the trees and buildings so fast that my fur stood on end. *Squeak!* Then I swooped **down**, **down**, **down**, diving between the cars, trucks, and motorcycles, right into the heart of the city: Swiss Square.

I **fLeW oVeR** the square and—

What was going on?!

A crowd of rodents was **scurrying** around below me. There was a lot of noise and an enormouse amount of confusion, but most of all—*gulp*—there was an **army** marching closer by the second!

I **DOVe** down to meet Swiftpaws (that's

Hercule's Heromouse alter ego). He was peering around the square.

By the power of Parmesan, there was no time to waste!

"Welcome, Superstilton!" Swiftpaws said, calm as can be.

"How can you be so *relaxed*?" I cried, quaking in my fur. "Let's get moving!"

He looked at me like my brain was full of fondue. "**WHAT?**"

My whiskers twitched. "I said, 'Let's get moving!'"

"Are you nervous, Superstilton?"

"Well, of course I am!" I yelped, twisting my tail into a knot. "Isn't the city in danger?!"

"Powerful provolone!"

Swiftpaws said with a laugh. "Of course

not, partner — the city is just beginning its celebration!"

I shook my snout. "Celebration?"

"**YEAH!** Look over there." Swiftpaws pointed to the middle of the square.

I *looked* to the right and saw tables piled with the tastiest cheese delicacies.

Strange . . .

I *looked* up and saw garlands and flags hanging over our heads.

Very strange . . .

I *looked* to the left and saw a stage set up for Mayor Pete Powerpaws's official speech.

Superstrange . . .

Finally, I *looked* in front of me and saw the army entering the square. But wait one mousely minute — that wasn't an **ARMY**!

That was . . . Muskrat City's *marching band*!

Super Swiss slices, how could I have mistaken it for an army? I felt like such a superfool!

"So, Superstilton, today Muskrat City is celebrating the birth of Pierre Poirat," Swiftpaws said.

I tried to focus on what Swiftpaws was saying. "Pierre **WHO**?"

"Pierre Poirat! My great-grandfather—the fearless Masked Mouse, the FIRST Heromouse called to defend the city from the terrible Sewer Rats!"

Suddenly . . .

Da–dada–daaaa!

A trumpet's blare loudly announced the start of the festivities, making my whiskers tremble in **shock**.

Da-dada-daaaa!

Then the band began to play, the crowd started to dance, and colored streamers **rained** down, covering the square.

Just then **TESS TECHNOPAWS**, the supersmart scientist and cook who works at Heromice Headquarters, pushed to the front of the crowd. Electron and Proton, the Heromice's two young helpers, were with her.

"Welcome, **SUPERSTILTON**!" Electron said.

"Did you **TASTE** the Gorgonzola

sandwiches?" Proton asked, passing me a tray of **cheesy** delicacies.

I reached for the tray with my paw, mouth watering. I was about to bite into the most enormouse sandwich I'd ever seen when I noticed a *FASCINATING* rodent nearby. She had blond hair, **BLUE EYES**, and wore a **blue suit**. It was Priscilla Slice, one of the most famouse, smart, and confident lawyers in **MUSKRAT CITY**!

And she was headed right toward me!

"Good afternoon, Superstilton!" Priscilla said with a smile, looking me *straight* in the eyes. "Have you been here long?"

Gulp!

"No . . . I mean . . . yes . . . well . . . I just got here!" I stammered, confused. I could feel that I'd turned as red as the sauce on a double-cheese pizza. Great Gouda gobs, why couldn't I play it **cool**?

But the more I looked at Priscilla, the more she reminded me of someone—oh, **of course**! Priscilla looked similar to the mouserific **Lady Wonderwhiskers**, the Heromouse who had stolen my **heart**!

Good afternoon!

While I was lost in thought, someone passing by shoved me. I tumbled to the ground with a **THUMP**.

"Hey, be careful!" I cried.

But when I picked myself up off the floor, Priscilla was gone. Super Swiss slices, **nothing** was going right for me today! Not even the thought of Lady

Wonderwhiskers could make it better.

I decided to **CONSOLE MYSELF** by finally biting into my mouthwatering triple Gorgonzola sandwich. But as I did, the crowd fell silent, the band stopped playing, and a familiar rodent appeared in the center of the square . . .

"ELENA SLUDGE!" Swiftpaws cried. "What are you doing here?"

INVASION OF THE SUPERPLANTS

A cold silence fell over the crowd. All **EYES** were focused on Elena Sludge.

"What are you looking at?" the young Sewer Rat snapped.

"Um . . ." Commissioner Rex Ratford, leader of the Muskrat City police, muttered.

"Can't a mouse even walk around the city in peace?" Elena asked **sharply**.

Elena was the daughter of **Tony Sludge**, the head of the stinky Sewer Rats. They live underground in a place called Rottington. But today Elena was in Muskrat City—and that meant trouble. Commissioner Ratford surely wouldn't let her **out** of his sight for a second!

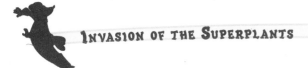
Everyone in the square around me was mostly going back to NORMAL, but all the mice avoided Elena as if she were a slice of massively moldy cheese. All of them—**except for one**.

Proton timidly approached the young Sewer Rat. "Umm, h-hi, Elena! Is ev-everything okay?"

"Proton, what are you doing?" Electron squeaked, trying to stop him. He waved her away with one paw.

PIERRE POIRAT

Hi, Elena!

Proton? What are you doing?

Elena looked at him with narrowed eyes. "What do you want?"

Proton didn't say anything. He just stood there with his mouth open. Oh, for the love of cheese, the poor mouselet was suddenly **squeakless**!

"Why is Proton talking to that troublemaker?" **ELECTRON** burst out, annoyed. Then she took my paw and dragged me up to Elena. "Oh, Elena, can I introduce you to **SUPERSTILTON**? Or maybe you know each other already?"

"**HmPH**," Elena grumbled. "I think I know of him . . ."

"Y-yes, we've met," I said awkwardly. Of course she knew me—I was always trying to put a stop to her father's **superslimy** plans!

Elena turned her back on me and looked at

Proton.

"You know, I've been sooooo busy these last few days."

"Really?" Proton said. "Well, I—I know you're REALLY good at chemistry, and so I wanted to ask . . . what are you working on now?"

"This!" Elena said suddenly, pulling a vial full of strange purple liquid out of her bag. She quickly POURED a few drops of the mysterious liquid in the flower beds lining Swiss Square. A moment later,

Ha-ha!

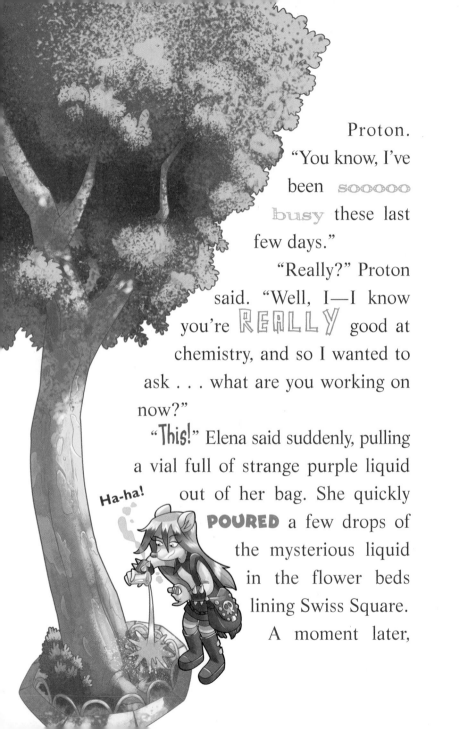

the trees in the square began to **grow, and grow, and grow** until they became truly enormouse! The roots poked out into the square—

Crack!—

while the branches extended like snakes.

"Mighty mozzarella, what's happening?" Swiftpaws exclaimed.

But before we could do anything . . . **pop!**

The sewer covers all over the square popped off, and out of the sewer came **Tony Sludge**, leader of the Sewer Rats, in his elegant dark suit; Teresa Sludge, the boss's

wife; SLICKFUR, Tony's slimy assistant; and ONE, TWO, and THREE, Tony's huge bodyguards.

"Good afternoon, Muskrattians!" Tony thundered. "I see you've already met my SUPERPLANTS!"

"Hold it right there!" Swiftpaws cried. "Clear these perilous plants away, or you will have to answer to the HEROMICE!"

Tony chuckled menacingly. "Not a chance, scaredy-mice. The fun has just begun!"

"Superstilton, are you ready?" my partner asked. "Let's remind these **SEWER RATS** not to mess with the Heromice!"

"**Um . . . are you sure?**" I muttered. My whiskers were trembling in fright!

Good afternoon, Muskrattians!

"Of course, partner!" Swiftpaws said, patting me on the shoulder. "Have courage.

HEROMICE IN ACTION!"

I sighed and gathered my strength.

I only knew one **thing** for sure: Sewer Rats plus superplants promised **supertrouble**!

Tony's Threat

Without a moment to waste, Swiftpaws **ran** toward Elena, but she was faster. She whispered something to a nearby sunflower and—THWACK!—the sunflower slapped my partner across the snout with its SUPERPETALS!

Swiftpaws began to sneeze. "Great Gouda! I'm—Achoo!—allergic—Achoo! Achoo!—to pollen! Achoo, achoo, achooo!"

I didn't know what to do. After all, I'm not cut out to be a Heromouse! I can admit it: I'm really a superscaredy-mouse at heart!

LUCKILY, at that very moment, the marvelmouse Lady Wonderwhiskers popped out of a nearby alley. With an incredible leap, my favorite heroine **launched** herself at One, Two, and Three and knocked them flat on their snouts!

I'm coming for you!

"I hope you don't mind," said the **fascinating** rodent, turning to me calmly. "But I was passing by and thought I would give you a paw!"

I was **dazed**, and my whiskers were wobbling. The

Argh!

fabumouse **Lady Wonderwhiskers** had arrived just in time!

I lost myself in her **EYES** . . . and they reminded me of someone. But who?

"**CAREFUL, SUPERSTILTON!**" Lady Wonderwhiskers squeaked, interrupting my daydream.

Oh no! While I was lost in thought, a giant ivy branch had *twisted* around one of my paws. It lifted me right off the ground!

"**HEEEEELP!**"

I *turned* and **THRASHED** in the plant's tight grip.

Whoosh! Whoosh!

I bumped my tail on a parked car.

THUMP! THUMP! THUMP!

I was flung onto the tables at a cute café.

CRASH!

I rolled down the street like a bowling ball.

Rumble!

Finally, I ended up whisker-deep in the middle of the thousand-cheese cheesecake!

"**Heroic Havarti**, Superstilton!" Swiftpaws yelled. "Does this seem like snack time? We're on a mission!"

Then Swiftpaws snapped into action. "Costume: Flying Disk Mode!"

A moment later, my partner transformed into an enormouse yellow disk. Then he spun through the air toward **ONE**, **TWO**, and **THREE**, who had just scrambled to their paws. They fell flat on their snouts again!

"*Nice shot, Swiftpaws!*" Lady Wonderwhiskers cried, running over to tie up the criminals as nimbly as a mouse playing with string cheese.

Unfortunately, we still hadn't dealt with ELENA.

"Geranium, attack!" she cried wickedly.

Within seconds, a GIANT climbing geranium immobilized Lady Wonderwhiskers, squeezing her in a bundle of branches and leaves.

Supersharp cheddar chunks, I had to do something!

"Hang on, Lady Wonderwhiskers!" I cried. "HERE I COME!"

With a heroic leap, I launched myself at the giant geranium. It hit me with one of its leaves and knocked me straight into the statue of Pierre Poirat . . . which was surrounded by superprickly thorn bushes!

Swiftpaws tried to intervene, but Slickfur aimed a giant gadget at him and stopped him in his tracks. "You're done, superfool!"

SUPERSTINKY
MANURE
LAUNCHER

"It's going to take a lot more than that to **STOP ME**, Slickfur!" Swiftpaws cried.

"We'll see about that!" Slickfur scoffed.

PLOOOF!

Just then a stream of superstinky manure **BLOCKeD** Swiftpaws's path, immobilizing him. Great gobs of Gouda, how *disgusting*! Luckily, Lady Wonderwhiskers had somehow *escaped* the clutches of the supergeranium. She ran to help Swiftpaws — but she was intercepted by Teresa Sludge.

"Ooooh, it looks like you're in quite a hurry," said Mrs. Sludge smoothly. "But wouldn't it be nice to stop and talk about this **snout-to-snout**?"

"Don't fall for it, Lady Wonderwhiskers!"

File No. 240455
Teresa Sludge

Who: Tony Sludge's wife

Where she lives: Teresa lives with her family in the subterranean fortress of Rottington, the stinky Sewer Rat headquarters.

Distinguishing traits: She can speak for hours without stopping, is obsessed with cleaning, and has hypnotic powers that she uses to fight the Heromice.

yelled SWIFTPAWS. "Get away from there—do **not** look at her!"

But it was too late!

Teresa had already locked her horrible **hypnotic stare** on Lady Wonderwhiskers.

"I feel so strange. What's happening?" Lady Wonderwhiskers muttered. "I'm so tired . . ."

"Keep looking at me," Teresa said calmly.

"Don't you feel like taking a little **nap**?"

Poor Lady Wonderwhiskers was **fading** fast under the influence of Teresa's stare.

"Oh, yes . . . I . . . really . . . want . . . to . . . take . . . a . . . long . . . snooze . . ."

ZZZ . . . ZZZ . . . ZZZ . . .

Super Swiss slices! I watched, helpless, as the rodent who had captured my **heart** fainted into **Slickfur's** evil paws.

"Ha, ha, ha!" hissed Teresa. "Did you see that, supergoons? Lady Wonderwhiskers is our prisoner now!"

"And let's be honest — **CAPTURING** her was as simple as leading a

Look into my eyes!

Gulp!

mouse to cheese!" Slickfur added.

I **twisted** my tail into a knot. "Let her go, or you'll pay!" I **SQUEAKED** with all the courage I could muster.

"Are you still up there, you ridiculous rodent?" Tony sneered, turning his snout toward me. "Let me guess—you can't get **down**?"

I was, in fact, still stuck at the top of PIERRE POIRAT'S statue. *Gulp!* Not only was it supertall (Did I mention that I'm afraid of heights?), but any time I tried to move my **paws**, I ended up pricking myself on some thorns!

What was a Heromouse to do?

"Ha, ha, ha!" Tony said with a sneer. "If you ever want to see your friend safe and sound again, surrender the city to us."

"NEVER!"

Commissioner Ratford said firmly. "We WiLL neVeR maKe a Pact WitH you SeWeR Rats!"

"Oh, really, Commissioner?" Tony replied, narrowing his eyes. "Listen to me: We will **give you** twelve hours to consider our offer. After that, we'll start spraying the superstinky manure again. The entire city will become an impenetrable jungle—a kingdom for the Sewer Rats! It will be the end of **MUSKRAT CITY**!"

And with that, the Sewer Rats disappeared underground into the sewers, carrying poor Lady Wonderwhiskers with them . . .

INTO THE SEWERS!

Swiftpaws hollered up at me. "Be brave, partner! **COME DOWN FROM THERE!**"

"But . . . well . . . I . . ." I tried to say, looking down. "It seems a bit dangerous."

"Leave it to me!" he said. "*Costume: Life Net Mode!*"

A moment later, Swiftpaws's costume turned into a large yellow life net, just like the ones used by firemice.

"Jump, Superstilton!" he cried.

I was **quaking** in my fur. "D-d-do I have to?"

"Trust me!" Swiftpaws called confidently.

I **sighed**. I didn't have a choice. I couldn't stay up there forever!

D-d-do I have to?

I covered my eyes, stepped forward, and . . .

thwomp!

I landed safe and sound in the **soft**, bouncy net.

Whew!

After that close encounter with the Sewer Rats and

their **superplants**, there was only one thing I wanted — to go back home to New Mouse City. And fast!

But unfortunately, SWIFTPAWS seemed to have other plans.

"Are you ready, Superstilton?" he asked.

"Wait a minute," I said, my tail twitching. "Ready for what?"

"Wake up, partner! We need to rescue Lady Wonderwhiskers! We can't leave her in the paws of the SLIMY and SINISTER Sewer Rats!"

Squeak! The thought of following those stinky rotten rats into the sewers of ROTTINGTON made my whiskers tremble, but Swiftpaws was right.

I gathered my COURAGE and squeezed my partner's paw.

"Heromice in action!" I cried.

Without a moment to waste, Swiftpaws and I **LOWERED** ourselves down through an open drain cover. The sewers were humid, moldy, and extremely stinky. Plus, they were so DARK that I wouldn't have been able to tell a cat from a rat!

After a while, we spotted some lights up ahead . . .

Mighty mozzarella, they were TORCHES. The Sewer Rats were headed our way!

Swiftpaws told me to cover my ears. Then he transformed his supersuit into an **ENORMOUSE** police siren.

Weeeee-ooooo! Weeeee-ooooo!

Weeeee-ooooo-weeeee-ooooo-weeeee-ooooo!

"Boss, what was that?" asked **ONE**, **TWO**, and **THREE** together.

A moment later, Swiftpaws transformed himself into a large *floodlight* that hit the Sewer Rats with a bright, powerful beam.

Hop! Hop!

"Huh? The police?" The three bodyguards grumbled in alarm, covering their eyes with their paws.

"Surrender!" Swiftpaws yelled.

Suddenly, we were face-to-face with **SLICKFUR**. Great Gouda! He pointed his terrible manure launcher directly at us and doused us with *superstinky* manure!

One, Two, and Three took advantage of our surprise to begin their attack, splashing through the putrid canal toward us.

Squish! Squish! Squish!

"Superstilton, we need a SUPER idea!" Swiftpaws exclaimed. "Costume: Superbellows Mode!"

After transforming himself into a yellow bellow designed to produce big gusts of air,

Swiftpaws began to blow as hard as he could. The *superwind* lifted up a superwave of mud — which hit the Sewer Rats square in their snouts!

"You superpests!" Tony Sludge hollered. "You ruined my new suit! Now show your snouts, if you're **brave** enough!"

We took a few slow steps forward.

When Tony saw us, he chuckled. "I can't believe you fell for that!"

Huh?

Slickfur pulled a remote from his pocket and pounded his paw on a red button. Two enormouse steel sheets *fell* from the ceiling and blocked our path. We couldn't go forward or backward.

"**OH NO!**" Swiftpaws squeaked in panic. We're **TRAPPED**!"

"Now what?" I whispered, trembling.

"See you later, superduds!" **Tony** snarled from the other side of the barrier.

Holey cheese! We were trapped in the middle of the muddy sewer with **NO WAY** out!

"Look, **SUPERSTILTON**!"

I lifted my snout and immediately turned as pale as a ball of mozzarella.

A tube overhead was pouring putrid water into the canal . . . and the *dirt* and **sludge** all around us was quickly rising. *Gulp!* Soon it would completely flood our little underground prison!

Holey heroic cheese balls! We were dangerously close to losing our fur!

UP TO OUR TAILS IN WATER

Swiftpaws and I looked around frantically, trying to find a way out. "Any superideas, SUPERSTILTON? We need to get out of here right away!"

I shrugged, feeling helpless.

Swiftpaws looked like he was going to pull out his whiskers. "But you're the journalist!" he said. "You're the *creative* one!"

"Yes, but I write my **books** in front of the fireplace," I pointed out. "I don't spend a lot of time in **stinky** sewers with filthy, soaking wet fur!"

As we talked, the mud around us was rising and rising.

Soon it would be up to our **whiskers**!

"Superstilton, I want to tell you something," Swiftpaws squeaked. "You're the **BesT** friend and partner a Heromouse could have."

I clapped him on the shoulder. "Swiftpaws, even if you always get me in **trouble**, I feel the same about you!"

Swiftpaws sighed.

"Good-bye, dear Superstilton . . ."

Wait just one minute!

We couldn't give up yet. Heromice **never** give up!

"Oh no!" I said suddenly. "By the power of putrid Parmesan, we won't go down this way!"

At those words, my **SUPER CHEESE POWERS** activated. A huge chunk of Parmesan cheese appeared, blocking the tube in the ceiling! The icky water stopped flowing, the mud stopped rising, and Swiftpaws and I both breathed a **HUGE** sigh of relief.

"**WE'RE SAVED!**" I rejoiced.

SUPERPOWER: SUPERSTOPPER MADE OF PARMESAN CHEESE ACTIVATED WITH THE CRY: "BY THE POWER OF PUTRID PARMESAN!"

"Hang on a minute, partner," Swiftpaws said. "We're still TRAPPED!"

Hmmm — he was right!

Suddenly, Swiftpaws let out a squeak, "Superstilton, did you see how these things are held in place?"

He pointed to the reinforced steel walls that BLOCKED our path. Looking closely, I could see that they were mounted with gigantic SCREWS and bolts.

Swiftpaws hollered,

"Costume: Screwdriver Mode!"

With that, we slowly began to loosen the screws — but, holey cheese, it wasn't easy!

"Huff . . . puff . . . pant!" I breathed heavily,

trying to help my partner out. "You're a genius, Swiftpaws, but these screws just won't budge."

"**We can do this!**" Swiftpaws said, determined. "Faster, partner!"

I worked as fast as I could. Finally, I loosened the last screw and . . .

CLANG!

The steel sheet fell to the ground. I couldn't believe my eyes. We were **free**!

The bad news was that there wasn't a trace of the Sewer Rats or their prisoner, Lady Wonderwhiskers. Where could they have taken her? My whiskers TREMBLED in fear just thinking about it.

"I think we need help from Tess,

ELECTRON, and Proton," I said.

"Definitely," Swiftpaws agreed. "But first we need to get cleaned up!"

With that, we dragged our stinky, sludgy fur back to Heromice Headquarters.

HUDDLING AT HEADQUARTERS

At Heromice Headquarters, I took a ratastic **shower** with some supersudsy Gorgonzola shampoo. Then I dried off with Tess's portable **fur dryer**—a truly **extraordinary** invention!

PORTABLE FUR DRYER

Meanwhile, Proton and Electron were trying to understand what had happened to the giant **plants** in Swiss Square.

Electron was busy **analyzing** a giant ivy

leaf under the microscope. She had picked it up after the **SEWER RATS'** attack, and now she was coming up with some hypotheses about how the plant had grown to be so enormouse.

"Elena must have created a **fast-acting supermanure** to use as fertilizer!" Electron concluded.

"I told you she was special," Proton said dreamily.

Electron rolled her eyes at him. "She might be **special**, but she'll never pull one over on us. We'll find the antidote to her supermanure and **save** Muskrat City! Right, guys?"

"**YEAH!**" Swiftpaws agreed. "We'll clean up the superplants and free **Lady Wonderwhiskers**!"

"If we only knew where they took her,"

I said, *sighing*.

At that moment, Tess Technopaws entered the room with a platter. "You'll think better on a full stomach. Why don't you all **munch** on something?"

I hadn't eaten in hours, so I dove into the sandwiches snoutfirst.

"Mozzarella and tomato?" I squeaked. **"YUM!"**

"Tess, you really are the best," Swiftpaws said, giving her a kiss on the paw.

Tess grinned. "And you are always a gentlemouse, Swiftpaws!"

Then the brilliant scientist and cook pulled something out of the pocket of her apron. "This is my latest invention. I thought you all might find it useful in your fight against the **Sewer Rats**!"

Tess showed us an object that looked like

a **FANCY** butterfly-shaped pin.

Swiftpaws observed it carefully. "Well, that's very **pretty**. But what are we supposed to do with a **butterfly pin**?"

Tess chuckled. "It's not a pin, Swiftpaws!" She brushed the head of the butterfly, and it began to bat its **COLORFUL** wings faster and faster.

Swiftpaws tried to shoo away the butterfly as it fluttered around his snout. "Um, interesting," he said. "It seems like a real butterfly!"

"*Cosmic cheddar chunks, no!*" Tess said. "It's not a butterfly—it's a butterflaser!"

"A butter-*what*?" Swiftpaws asked,

shaking his snout in confusion.

In answer, the **butterflaser** emitted a subtle red ray that zapped my partner's tail.

"Ouccech!"

Ouccch!

The butterflaser continued to show off its **POWERS**—and poor Swiftpaws was forced to hide under the table.

"Never underestimate Tess Technopaws's inventions!" Proton said with a giggle.

Tess smiled. "When you brush it on the head, the butterflaser emits microscopic laser rays."

"**Microscopic** but brutal!" Swiftpaws said with a groan. "Ouch!"

"It's a *FANTASTIC* invention, Tess!" I said, taking the butterflaser and pinning it to my chest.

"**Heromice**, look!" Electron cut in, raising the volume on the television.

We all turned to the screen, where a special edition of the news had just started. The newscaster, Chatty McCheddar, seemed worried.

"Good afternoon, Muskrat TV viewers. After the surprise appearance of the Sewer Rats in Swiss Square this morning, more trouble has been brewing at the Botanic Garden. It seems that the situation has gotten out of control. The plants there have transformed into gigantic superplants! According to some witnesses, the Sewer Rats have also been seen at the Botanic Garden . . . and not with peaceful intentions. Here is a video taken with a bystander's cell phone."

As we watched the news report, our mouths fell open. The Botanic Garden had become a **JUNGLE**!

Heroic Havarti!

Elena's superstinky manure had struck again!

"**Come on**, Superstilton!" Swiftpaws exclaimed. "We need to get to the Botanic Garden immediately! Im-me-di-ate-ly!"

"B-but maybe—" I stammered.

"Do you have cheese in your **EARS**, Superstilton?" Swiftpaws tugged on my paw impatiently. "Let's go!"

"N-no, I mean, yes . . . I mean . . . why

don't we finish **eating** first?" I responded, trying to stall.

I'll say it again: I AM JUST NOT CUT OUT TO BE A HEROMOUSE!

"Enough chitchat, my friend—the destiny of **MUSKRAT CITY** is in our paws!" Swiftpaws yelled.

We darted out of Heromice Headquarters at *supersonic speed*. I barely heard Tess squeak after us.

"Good luck, **HEROMICE**!" she said. "While you're at the Botanic Garden, we'll keep looking for the **antidote** to Elena's superstinky manure . . ."

DANGER AT THE BOTANIC GARDEN

After a *SUPERSPEEDY* flight, we arrived at the gates of the Muskrat City Botanic Garden.

The scene before our eyes was **incredible**: There were roses as tall as buildings, vines as long as bridges, and fLOWeRS as big as billboards!

Gulp!

I still felt all *topsy-turvy* from flying. It was like my stomach was in my tail, and my tail was in my whiskers, and my whiskers were in my paws. Ugh!

AND UNFORTUNATELY I HAD A FEELING THAT THE WORST WAS YET TO COME!

"W-what should we do? W-we don't need to go into the middle of all that, right?" I asked SWIFTPAWS, pointing to the tangle of superplants ahead of us.

"Remember, SUPERSTILTON—a real Heromouse has no fear," said Swiftpaws, superconfident as usual.

My stomach did a flip-flop. "Umm, b-but I'm afraid of *everything*! You know that I'm not—"

"Superstilton, now is not the time to **freeze up**! We need to find Lady Wonderwhiskers before it's too late!"

I sighed. Entering that maze of extra-large, extra-scary plants made my whiskers **tremble**, but helping Lady Wonderwhiskers was the most important thing. I would do *anything* to save her!

"Let's split up," Swiftpaws said to me.

"One of us will go on a reconnaissance flight . . ."

Another flight? I shuddered.

"Great! You go right ahead!" I squeaked.

"Actually, **SUPERSTILTON**, I think you should do it," Swiftpaws said.

"Me? Why me?"

"Because you are a Heromouse," my partner said. "And whether you like it or not, I **know** you can do it."

Whoaaaa!

Maybe, just maybe, Swiftpaws was right. Like it or not, I was a Heromouse, and a Heromouse never gives up! Or at least, a Heromouse **shouldn't** ever give up!

I concentrated as hard as I could and ROSE UP off the ground. I was flying!

From above, I couldn't **SEE** much of anything except a thick barrier of superplants covering the **Botanic Garden**. A wisp of smoke drifted through the tangle of leaves, branches, and petals, curling into the sky.

Mighty mozzarella, did the Sewer Rats really light a fire right in the middle of the Botanic Garden?

I zipped back down to the ground and told Swiftpaws what I had seen.

Suddenly, our wrist communicators crackled. *"Heromice, do you hear me? Go by land!"* Tess's voice cried through the speakers.

I froze. "By land? D-do we have to?"

But before I could even twitch my tail, Swiftpaws had already run into the heart of that scary superplant forest. Powerful provolone, he was *fast*!

I bolted into the dark to catch up with him, and I felt Swiftpaws put a paw on my shoulder.

"Let's stick TOGETHER," I squeaked.

But when Swiftpaws responded, his voice sounded far away. "What was that, **SUPERSTILTON**? I'm over here!"

Wait just a second . . . **then who — or what — had just touched me**?!

I turned around, and . . .

"HELP!"

An enormouse slimy green vine wrapped itself around me and lifted me off the ground! SWIFTPAWS darted toward me, but an even bigger, slimier, greener vine **hit** him like a whip, flinging him away.

Wa-chhhhh!

"You superplants are a superpain!" he cried. "Costume: Garden Shears Mode!"

Just then Electron's voice on the wrist communicator stopped him in his tracks. *"Stop, Swiftpaws! You can't shear those poor plants! They can't help it if they were transformed . . ."*

How rude!

"What do you mean, '**poor plants**'? Poor *me*!" Swiftpaws exclaimed. "What should I do instead?"

At that moment, a *vine* wrapped itself around his waist and began to squeeze.

"This isn't going well!" he said. "*Costume: Robot Ladybug Mode!*"

In a flash, my partner transformed into a **tiny** yellow robotic ladybug and slipped right out of the vine's grasp, sticking out his tongue at it. **PFFFFFT!**

Swiftpaws laughed. "A **small** but mouserific idea!"

"Okay, now think of something for me!" I yelled. "*Great globs of melty mozzarella*, I'm still stuck up here!"

At those words, my cheesy superpowers activated again. In the twitch of a tail, a rainstorm of soft, gooey mozzarella globs

Heeeeeelppppp!

struck the vine that was about to crush me. The vine let go, and I fell to the ground, landing hard on my tail. YOUCH!

I may have been bruised—but I was safe!

"Good job, Superstilton!" Swiftpaws said. "See that? Nothing is impossible for the Heromice!"

ELENA STRIKES AGAIN!

SWIFTPAWS and I continued our trek through the garden until we found ourselves at the edge of a carpet of fallen leaves. Everything was completely *silent*. It seemed like there was no one around. Until . . .

"Ooooh, the **superfools** are here!" said a voice above us.

Our snouts snapped up. Sitting on the branch of a **giant** oak overhead was none other than Elena Sludge.

"Are you ready to take on my supermushrooms?" the SNEAKY Sewer Rat asked smugly.

We looked around, but there were no signs of mushrooms.

BOING! I had spoken too soon!

Elena dumped her superstinky manure on the ground, and a few moments later . . .

BOING! BOING! BOING!

A line of giant **SUPERMUSHROOMS** sprouted up under our paws!

Swiftpaws and I bounced like balls in a

pinball machine as we were **tossed** from one mushroom to the next!

BOING! BOING! BOING!

Finally, my partner took to the air, scooping me up, too.

"Don't tell me that you don't like mushrooms," Elena said with a **snicker**.

"The only mushrooms I like are the ones on an extra-cheese pizza!" I said.

Just then a nearby **SUPERMUSHROOM** bumped my tail.

"Could it be that the *Sewer Rats* are just too strong for you?" Elena asked.

"What did you say?" Swiftpaws cried incredulously.

Elena chuckled. "You would be better off giving up!"

"The Heromice never give up!" I responded with all the courage I could muster.

"Good one, Superstilton!" Swiftpaws said with a determined nod.

I was still as terrified as a mouse in a cottage full of cats, but the thought of Lady Wonderwhiskers in danger gave me fabumouse strength—a **special**

strength that allowed me to face my fears snout-on!

Elena suddenly disappeared among the branches, but I had a feeling we hadn't seen the last of her. We hurried away from the **SUPERMUSHROOMS**, but the surprises weren't over yet!

"What could **that** be?" Swiftpaws asked after a moment, coming to a stop.

We were facing a wall of wild roses and thorny shrubs.

Gulp! Just looking at it made my whiskers tremble and my fur stand on end!

EVERY ROSE HAS ITS THORNS

We tried to walk into the enormouse rose garden, but the plants were so **THICK** that we couldn't get anywhere.

Swiftpaws grabbed my arm. "I have an idea, partner—let's fly overhead."

Before I could answer, my partner zoomed into the air, **DRAGGING** me with him.

"Make sure we keep a safe distance from the thorns!" SWIFTPAWS warned, pointing.

I shuddered. "Well, since those roses have thorns the size of **GIGANTIC NEEDLES**, that's probably a good idea." Suddenly, I yelped. "Yow! What was that?"

Supersharp cheddar chunks, the wild roses were reaching up to prick our tails!

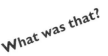
What was that?

"Swiftpaws, they're attacking us!" I squeaked.

"Wait here," he said urgently. "I'll try to fly over the rose garden at top speed and distract them. When I get to the other side, follow me!"

"But couldn't we find **another** way through?" I asked, hovering in the air uncertainly.

"Superstilton, are you or are you not a Heromouse?" my friend asked.

I frowned and stayed put as Swiftpaws flew at supermousetastic speed above the rose garden.

But before he could reach the other side, his **costume** snagged on a giant thorn.

"*Mighty mozzarella!*" he cried. "Help, Superstilton!"

I flew forward a few feet, but the thorns kept reaching up to jab me. "*Ahhh! Oooh! Yow!*" I yelped. "*For a thousand chunky cheese balls, this really hurts!*"

At those words, my incredible cheesy superpowers kicked into gear. The sky opened up, and a storm of **cheese balls** rained down!

Thousands of balls of **SOFT** mozzarella cheese rammed into the thorns. Suddenly, those thorns were completely harmless!

I took advantage of the break in the action to **free** Swiftpaws. Then we flew to a spot far away from the nightmarish thicket

of roses and thorns. Whew—another narrow escape!

"Thanks, **SUPERSTILTON**," Swiftpaws said. "I never would have made it without you!"

But there was no time to rest. We had to keep searching for Lady Wonderwhiskers and the Sewer Rats! We passed a forest of asparagus as tall as redwood trees, CROSSED a stream that smelled like chives, and finally found ourselves in front of a lake surrounded by gigantic dandelions.

"Time to fly, partner!" Swiftpaws said, taking off like a rocket.

But at that moment, One, Two, and

Three — Tony Sludge's bodyguards — lumbered out from behind the dandelions, waving ENORMOUSE fans. The huge, fluffy dandelion seeds filled the air, heading right for my partner.

"Careful, Swiftpaws!" I cried — but he had already flown right into a huge cloud of dandelion seeds.

Spuuut!
Spuuuuut!

"Super Swiss slices, I wasn't expecting that!" Swiftpaws sputtered.

Disoriented by the superdandelions, Swiftpaws lost control of his costume and

began to fall **doẅn, doẅn, doẅn** - - -

toward the lake below. He was about to be **soaked** like a ball of marinated provolone! Luckily, a gigantic **water lily** broke his fall.

FLUMP!

"Swiftpaws!" I **yelled** from the shore. "Are you still in one piece?"

"Of course!" Swiftpaws answered, standing up and rubbing his tail. "It will take more than that to **stop** a fearless Heromouse like me. *Costume: Motor Mode!*"

With that, he used the water

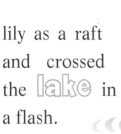

Oof!

lily as a raft and crossed the lake in a flash.

But I was still stuck on the opposite shore — and I was all alone!

"Be brave, **SUPERSTILTON**! Come on over!"

My whiskers wobbled. "Umm . . . I mean . . . I don't know if I can make it . . ."

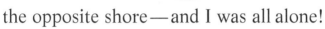

"You can do it!

My superintuition tells me that we're almost there!"

I had a bad feeling about this, but I couldn't let SWIFTPAWS down. And most of all, I couldn't abandon the fabumouse Lady Wonderwhiskers!

So I jumped on a **water lily**, too! Paddling with all my might, I finally reached the other side. Whew—even my tail was tired!

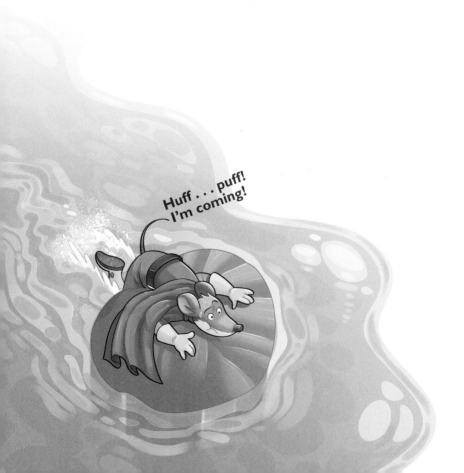

SHOWDOWN AT THE BOTANIC GARDEN

We had finally made it to the heart of the **Botanic Garden**, behind the tropical plant conservatory.

The Sewer Rats were there, and they had a fire blazing, with an enormouse cauldron on top.

"**What are they doing?**" Swiftpaws whispered.

I looked closely. "I think that's what **ELENA** uses to make her superstinky manure."

Powerful provolone, it looked like there was enough manure in the cauldron to transform the whole city into an **impenetrable jungle**!

Tony, Teresa, Elena, Slickfur, and **ONE**,

TWO, and THREE were all gathered around the fire. We spotted Lady Wonderwhiskers nearby, imprisoned between some giant tulip petals.

As soon as we stepped forward, she cried out in relief. "Superstilton! Swiftpaws! It's Fabumouse to see you!"

"It's about time, superfools!" Tony sneered, whirling around to face us. "We've been waiting for you."

"Are you ready for **prison**, you slimy Sewer Rats?" Swiftpaws asked.

My partner jumped in front of Tony but was immediately attacked by SLICKFUR and his messy manure launcher.

SPLat!

"You're too slow for this Heromouse, Fetid Fontina Face!" Swiftpaws hollered,

zigzagging
between the
shots of **superstinky
manure**.

Tony Sludge chuckled.
"Are you sure about
that?"

SPLAT!

This time, the manure
hit Swiftpaws straight
on—and he ended up
stuck to a tree trunk!

"Great gobs of Gouda!"
he yelped. "Do something,
SUPERSTILTON!"

Oh, cheese and
crackers! With Lady
Wonderwhiskers and
Swiftpaws both out

of the game, I was the only Heromouse left standing. The thought of it made my fur STAND ON END!

ELECTRON'S strong voice suddenly crackled through my wrist communicator. *"Good news, Superstilton! We did it!"*

I froze. "Uhh . . . did what?"

"We found the superstinky manure antidote! Hang on!"

"I'll do my best!" I responded. But Slickfur had already pointed his menacing manure launcher right at me. Gulp!

I avoided the first shot by lowering my head . . .

SPLAT!

I jumped up and avoided the second shot . . .

SPLAT!

The third shot missed me because I slipped on a giant leaf . . .

SPLAT!

And I turned that leaf into a shield to block myself from the fourth shot . . .

SPLAT!

"Hold still!" Slickfur yelled. "Let's get you nice and covered with manure!"

I wasn't going down without a fight. "In your dreams, **Havarti Head**!"

I turned to fly to safety, but because of a little problem during takeoff, I ended up **slamming** into a branch!

Bam!

I tried to straighten myself out, but I got caught on another branch.

Mighty mozzarella, what a day!

"You're done for, Heromice!" **SLICKFUR**

said, preparing to blast another shot of manure.

At the exact moment he shot the manure launcher, the branch snapped. I fell to the ground like a ten-pound chunk of Parmesan!

OOF!

I didn't have time to shake my snout or celebrate my escape before Elena scurried up to a werewolf daisy and whispered something to it.

A moment later, the plant opened its mouse-munching jaws and trapped me in its fanged petals!

A second werewolf daisy reached out and grabbed Swiftpaws, too.

OH NO! We were going to be minced mousemeat!

Now that the Heromice were all imprisoned by ravenous superplants, what would happen to Muskrat City?

"**THIS IS IT!**" Slickfur exclaimed with a **smile**. "Our fanged superplants will crush you in a single bite!"

Just then Tony lifted a **paw** and confidently turned to the rest of his gang.

Pssst . . . pssst . . . pssst . . .

"Are you ready to witness the end of **MUSKRAT CITY** as we know it?"

"Oh, Sludgy, I can't wait!" his wife, Teresa, squeaked, her eyes sparkling with **wickedness**.

"Good-bye, Heromice!" Tony sneered.

FLATTER THOSE FLOWERS!

Holey cheese, it was all over for us! We were done for, goners, *mincemice*!

It was getting awfully uncomfortable between the **fangs** of the werewolf daisy. I squirmed and kicked and thrashed my paws.

"LET ME GO! LET ME GO! LET ME GO!" I said desperately. "I don't want to be crumbled up like Feta!"

But the **superplant** had no intention of releasing me. Just then I got an idea . . .

Great Gouda, Aunt Sweetfur's advice! Why didn't I think of it before?

"I have an idea, Swiftpaws!" I shouted to my partner.

Swiftpaws squirmed in his werewolf daisy. "What are you waiting for? Tell me!"

"We need to talk to the plants—but **sweetly**. Aunt Sweetfur always says that talking to plants makes them haPPy!"

Swiftpaws looked at me like I was crazy. "Are you sure that will work?"

I nodded. "Trust me, SWIFTPAWS—we have no other choice!"

But my **partner** still didn't seem convinced.

I started to gently pat a leaf of the carnivorous plant. "What a fabumouse **GREEN** color! You're the most beautiful werewolf daisy in the whole universe!"

The **monstrous** superplant loosened its grip a bit, so I continued. "You're strong, and your teeth are so clean, so white, and so SHiNY!"

GULP! If this plan didn't work, I had a feeling I'd be getting an even closer look at those teeth!

Luckily, the werewolf daisy was flattered and let go—and I was able to escape! Swiftpaws's jaw dropped. Right away, he used the same technique to save himself.

But I couldn't focus on him because the werewolf daisy I had escaped from kept looking at me sweetly! Oops . . . I may have done too good a job flattering that plant!

"Does this seem like the best time to turn plants into your best friends, partner?" Swiftpaws said. "We have a mission to complete!"

"I'm coming!" I cried.

But before I could move a mousely muscle . . .

"Those supergoons are still *alive*?" I heard Slickfur hiss from nearby.

Before Tony Sludge's assistant could do a thing, Lady Wonderwhiskers appeared out of nowhere and knocked Slickfur to the ground with an **amazing** kick. She had used my flattery tactic to free herself from the supertulip!

Well, I . . .

What a *tough* rodent!

Plus, she was so fascinating, charming, elegant, and beautiful . . .

101

"Thanks, Lady Wonderwhiskers!" Swiftpaws exclaimed, snapping me out of my thoughts. "You really saved our fur!"

"How can I **repay** you, Lady Wonderwhiskers?" I asked. "Perhaps I can make you a **delicious** dinner? Or a **homemade** cheesecake?"

"**Careful**, Superstilton!" Swiftpaws suddenly yelled.

Holey cheese, Tony Sludge was running right at me with the **manure launcher** in his paws!

Suddenly, I remembered Tess's awesome **butterflaser**.

I placed it on the ground and tapped its head. It began to **FLY** and flap its wings around Tony Sludge's **ugly** snout.

"**Shoo!**" Tony spat in annoyance. "Get lost, you **tiny** pest!"

A moment later, the butterflaser began to bombard **Tony** with its deadly precision lasers.

"Eek! Ack! Ugh!" Tony cried, jumping around and patting his *singed* fur.

Meanwhile, One, Two, and Three ran at Swiftpaws—but he had already turned into a giant **rubber** flyswatter! He swatted them all away.

BOING!
BOING!
BOING!

Meanwhile, Lady Wonderwhiskers had darted off after **ELENA** and Teresa.

"Get her!" Elena shouted, launching a vial full of *superstinky manure* at Lady Wonderwhiskers.

But Lady Wonderwhiskers was ready! She snatched the vial out of the air and continued her chase.

Teresa suddenly came to a stop. "I'll deal with this right here and now." Once again, she tried to *hypnotize* Lady Wonderwhiskers.

"I'm not going to fall for that this time!" our fellow Heromouse said, looking away from Teresa and hurling the vial of superstinky manure to the ground.

The manure splashed onto a bunch of oleander shrubs nearby. They grew supersized and created a giant barrier!

Teresa was on the other side, so she couldn't hypnotize Lady Wonderwhiskers with her magnetic gaze.

Lady Wonderwhiskers was such a clever rodent!

"Superstilton, look over there!" Swiftpaws said, tugging at my cape.

A police helicopter was **flying** overhead. "Surrender, Sewer Rats!" Commissioner Ratford bellowed from a megaphone inside the helicopter.

A second helicopter darted through the sky, spraying a strange greenish rain all over the **Botanic Garden**.

Super Swiss slices! As soon as the green drops hit the ground, the SUPERPLANTS went back to being regular old plants again.

"It's the antidote!" Swiftpaws

exclaimed. "Tess Technopaws and the mouselets did it!"

"**GREAT JOB, HEROMICE!**" said Commissioner Ratford when his helicopter landed nearby.

But there was no time to celebrate.

"Everyone to the **Sludgemobile**!" Tony Sludge shouted, heading for his armored limousine behind the tropical conservatory.

Electron and Proton clambered out of the helicopter, and Proton accidentally found himself snout-to-snout with ELENA again.

"Proton!" Swiftpaws shouted. "Stop her! Catch her!"

But Proton turned as red as a vat of cheesy marinara sauce. He couldn't move a paw!

As the Sewer Rats' armored supercar

dug a **tunnel** in the ground with its enormouse *superdrill*, Elena blew Proton a kiss from the window.

"See you soon, Proton! You may have **won** this time, but we'll meet **again**!"

Later!

B-b-bye, Elena!

There's No Place Like Home

A few hours later, **MUSKRAT CITY** was officially back to normal thanks to the special antidote. There were no more mushrooms as big as houses or trees as tall as skyscrapers!

Along with Tess Technopaws and the mouselets, Swiftpaws and I returned to where it had all started: Swiss Square.

"Mighty mozzarella!" Swiftpaws said with a sigh. "It seems impossible that just a few hours ago this square was a jungle of superplants."

"The Sewer Rats put up a tough fight this time," said Tess.

110

"But as long as the Heromice are on the job, Muskrat City can *sleep* peacefully," Electron added. "Isn't that right, Superstilton? Hey,

SUPERSTILTON?"

Huh? I hadn't heard a word my friends were saying. That's because not too far away, Muskrat TV was **interviewing** Priscilla Slice.

The more I watched her, the more she looked like someone I knew: that blond fur . . . those blue eyes . . . that pointy snout.

But who?

"Lady Wonderwhiskers is the best," Swiftpaws shouted. "Right, partner? I mean, without her, things would have gotten really **ugly**!"

"Um . . . **YES** . . . of course . . ." I muttered.

Just then Priscilla **turned** our way and greeted us with a nod.

"Wow, did you see that?" Swiftpaws said. "Priscilla was saying hi to me!"

I laughed. "No way! She was saying hi to me!"

Of course!

Will you give us an interview?

"**Powerful provolone**, you are so wrong!" my partner retorted.

"That's enough *fighting*!" said Tess, stepping between us and holding up a paw. "What do you say we all recharge with a little snack?"

She pulled two tiny capsules out of her bag, poured a bit of water on them, and — BAM!

We found ourselves in front of two piping hot trays of cheesy lasagna!

Tess grinned proudly. "This is my latest invention: miniaturized snack plates. *Delicious!*"

"*Cheesy lasagna!*" shouted Swiftpaws. "My favorite! Yum!"

I enjoyed a heaping plateful of lasagna in **silence**. Ah, how relaxing! It was almost SUNSET, and that meant it was time for me to go back to New Mouse City.

2) JUST ADD WATER

3) RESULT: A DELICIOUS DISH!

"See you soon, SWIFTPAWS," I said. "Despite everything, it was nice to fight for what's right alongside you, as always."

"Yeah, partner," he said with a GRIN. "You're not so bad yourself."

I hugged TESS, ELECTRON, and Proton, then took flight and headed toward New Mouse City.

My costume *sped* me through the sky like a bolt of lightning, then steered me toward the terrace of my house.

1) MINI CAPSULES

Ahhh . . . home sweet home!

But I had to say—*squeak!*—it seemed like the **costume** was making me fall at a supersonic speed!

"No, nooo, noooooooooo!"

Bonk!

"Owwwww!" I landed right on the spiky quills of one of my beloved **cacti**. What a way to end a flight!

I got up quickly—and painfully—with my tail covered in quills, but I let out a huge sigh of relief.

"You're awfully spiky, but **luckily**, you're a regular cactus!" I said with a grin.

I had seen it all during our latest adventure against the **superplants**. Now I was more convinced than ever that it really is important to be **sweet** to your plants!

I decided to pamper my little plants with some **FRESH WATER** and a good bedtime story, just like Aunt Sweetfur had suggested. As I whispered a *lullaby* to the daisies, the roses, and even the cacti, I thought about the **MISSION** I had just finished.

Once upon a time . . .

As I relived our incredibly fabumouse and fur-raising adventure, it became clear that

nothing is impossible for the Heromice!

DON'T MISS ANY HEROMICE BOOKS!

#1 Mice to the Rescue!

#2 Robot Attack

#3 Flood Mission

#4 The Perilous Plants

#5 The Invisible Thief

Be sure to read all my fabumouse adventures!

#1 Lost Treasure of the Emerald Eye

#2 The Curse of the Cheese Pyramid

#3 Cat and Mouse in a Haunted House

#4 I'm Too Fond of My Fur!

#5 Four Mice Deep in the Jungle

#6 Paws Off, Cheddarface!

#7 Red Pizzas for a Blue Count

#8 Attack of the Bandit Cats

#9 A Fabumouse Vacation for Geronimo

#10 All Because of a Cup of Coffee

#11 It's Halloween, You 'Fraidy Mouse!

#12 Merry Christmas, Geronimo!

#13 The Phantom of the Subway

#14 The Temple of the Ruby of Fire

#15 The Mona Mousa Code

#16 A Cheese-Colored Camper

#17 Watch Your Whiskers, Stilton!

#18 Shipwreck on the Pirate Islands

#19 My Name Is Stilton, Geronimo Stilton

#20 Surf's Up, Geronimo!

#21 The Wild, Wild West

#22 The Secret of Cacklefur Castle

A Christmas Tale

#23 Valentine's Day Disaster

#24 Field Trip to Niagara Falls

#25 The Search for Sunken Treasure

#26 The Mummy with No Name

#27 The Christmas Toy Factory

#28 Wedding Crasher

#29 Down and Out Down Under

#30 The Mouse Island Marathon

#31 The Mysterious Cheese Thief

Christmas Catastrophe

#32 Valley of the Giant Skeletons

#33 Geronimo and the Gold Medal Mystery

#34 Geronimo Stilton, Secret Agent

#35 A Very Merry Christmas

#36 Geronimo's Valentine

#37 The Race Across America

#38 A Fabumouse School Adventure

#39 Singing Sensation

#40 The Karate Mouse

#41 Mighty Mount Kilimanjaro

#42 The Peculiar Pumpkin Thief

#43 I'm Not a Supermouse!

#44 The Giant Diamond Robbery

#45 Save the White Whale!

#46 The Haunted Castle

#47 Run for the Hills, Geronimo!

#48 The Mystery in Venice

#49 The Way of the Samurai

#50 This Hotel Is Haunted!

#51 The Enormouse Pearl Heist

#52 Mouse in Space!

#53 Rumble in the Jungle

#54 Get into Gear, Stilton!

#55 The Golden Statue Plot

#56 Flight of the Red Bandit

The Hunt for the Golden Book

#57 The Stinky Cheese Vacation

#58 The Super Chef Contest

#59 Welcome to Moldy Manor

The Hunt for the Curious Cheese

#60 The Treasure of Easter Island

#61 Mouse House Hunter

#62 Mouse Overboard!

The Hunt for the Secret Papyrus

#63 The Cheese Experiment

DEAR MOUSE FRIENDS,
THANKS FOR READING, AND
FAREWELL TILL THE NEXT BOOK.
IT'LL BE ANOTHER
WHISKER-LICKING-GOOD
ADVENTURE, AND THAT'S
A PROMISE!